NORMAN BRIDWELL

Oops, Clifford!®

SCHOLASTIC INC.

New York   Toronto   London   Auckland   Sydney

ISBN 0-590-63117-9

12   11   10   9   8   7   6   5   8   9/9   0/0   01   02   03

Printed in the U.S.A.
First printing, September 1998

Hi! I'm Emily Elizabeth.

I have the biggest, reddest dog on our street.

This is my dog—Clifford.

Oh, I know he's not perfect.
He makes mistakes sometimes.

Clifford just doesn't know how big he is. One day, his pals found some pipes to play in. Clifford tried to follow them.

But he was too big.

The pipe was stuck on Clifford's nose and he couldn't see. Oops!

Luckily, the pipe came off.

When all the kids in town had a sack race, Clifford wanted to race, too. The coach said that all his feet had to be in one bag.

I found a sack that was big enough.

Then we were off!

Oops!

One day, Clifford and I were doing good deeds with our friend Tim. Somebody had let the air out of the tires of a car. The man asked if we could help him.

Tim took a rubber tube out of the car and stuck it on the tire valve. Then he told Clifford to blow air through the tube.

Clifford blew. Oops!

He blew a little too hard.

The man felt better
when he took his car to a garage.

Clifford also did a good deed when the circus
came to town. The owner said everything was
going wrong. He didn't think they could put
on the show.

I told him Clifford and I would help him. He didn't think a girl and her dog could be much help. But I said, "The show must go on."

Clifford put on a clown costume and joined
the act. Clifford enjoyed being a clown.

He wagged his tail. Oops!
That made the act even better.

One day, two nice police officers asked me about my dog.
I told them he could do tricks.

Then I told Clifford to roll over.

Oops! That was a mistake.

Later that day I saw a girl do a foolish thing. She was walking on the railing of a bridge.

Then she slipped.

Her dog tried to save her.

But he just wasn't big enough
or strong enough.
HELP! HELP! HELP!

Hooray for Clifford! He saved the girl.

The policemen were so happy that they forgave
Clifford for mashing their car.

Clifford may not be perfect . . . but I love him just the same!

Look for the pictures from **Oops, Clifford!** in these other funny books!

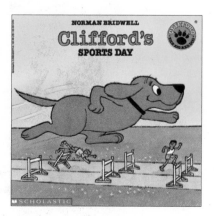

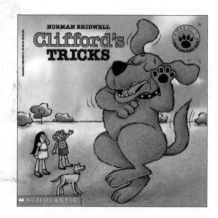

Happy reading!

Norman Bridwell's career got off to a big start with the publication of CLIFFORD THE BIG RED DOG. Thirty-six years and many books later, Mr. Bridwell continues to enchant the picture-book crowd.

What makes Clifford so irresistible? Mr. Bridwell has his own theory: "I think Clifford's success is based on his not being perfect. Clifford always tries to do the right thing, but he does make mistakes."

Norman Bridwell, who was born and raised in Indiana, lives in Martha's Vineyard, Massachusetts.